DK

STAR WARS

T0011400

JEDI

POCKET EXPERT

Written by Catherine Saunders

CONTENTS

HOW TO USE THIS BOOK

This book is organized alphabetically by first name, so use the contents list above to find the character you're looking for. Difficult words or terms are explained in the glossary on p.78, and below is a key to the abbreviations used for each character's appearances in the Key Facts box.

THR: The High Republic
I: Star Wars: Episode I The Phantom Menace
II: Star Wars: Episode II Attack of the Clones
CW: Star Wars: The Clone Wars animated TV series
BB: Star Wars: Bad Batch animated TV series
III: Star Wars: Episode III Revenge of the Sith
FO: Star Wars: Jedi: Fallen Order video game
R: Star Wars Rebels animated TV series
RO: Rogue One: A Star Wars Story

IV: Star Wars: Episode IV A New Hope
V: Star Wars: Episode V The Empire Strikes Back
VI: Star Wars: Episode VI Return of the Jedi
M: Star Wars: The Mandalorian TV series
VII: Star Wars: Episode VII The Force Awakens
VIII: Star Wars: Episode VIII The Last Jedi
IX: Star Wars: Episode IX The Rise of Skywalker

Yaddle

WHO ARE THE JEDI?

Good question! By the end of this book, you'll be an expert on all things Jedi. You'll meet some of the most famous Jedi of all time, celebrate some unsung heroes, and see where it all went wrong for a few who rejected their Jedi calling. You'll also learn how beings become Jedi, how the Jedi fight, and what the Force is.

OK, so back to your question: The Jedi are an ancient order whose purpose is to keep peace in

THE FORCE

The Force is an invisible energy that surrounds all living things. Jedi have a natural ability to use the power of the Force.

the galaxy and to uphold justice. They use the Force to help them solve problems, to defend others, and to resist evil. The Jedi follow a set of rules called the Jedi Code and are led by the Jedi Council, a group of the 12 wisest and most experienced Jedi. The Jedi Temple on Coruscant (below) is the headquarters of the Jedi. It is where young Jedi are trained, and where the Jedi Archives, containing centuries of knowledge, are located.

JEDI CODE

The most important part of the Jedi Code is self-discipline. Jedi must learn to control their feelings and not give in to anger, or love.

JEDI RANK

- ☐ Youngling
- ☐ Padawan
- ☐ Knight
- ☑ Master
- ☐ Grand Master

AAYLA SECURA

Athletic and agile, Jedi Master Aayla Secura is a skilled fighter. She is a brave and loyal Jedi who does everything she can to keep the citizens of the Galactic Republic safe.

Aayla holds her lightsaber in a battle-ready stance

Twi'leks can communicate using their lekku (head-tails)

KEY FACTS

Homeworld: Ryloth
Species: Twi'lek
Height: 1.7 m (5 ft 7 in)
Trained by: Quinlan Vos
Appearances: II, CW, III

JEDI FACT

Aayla helps Ahsoka Tano when the young Padawan is finding it hard to leave her Jedi Master, Anakin Skywalker.

JEDI GENERAL

During the Clone Wars, Aayla is a Jedi general and leads many missions. She stays in contact with her fellow Jedi via hologram.

ADI GALLIA

Adi Gallia is a member of the Jedi High Council. She is respected for her intuition and intelligence, and was the first Jedi to become aware of suspicious activity on Naboo.

Youngling ☐
Padawan ☐
Knight ☐
Master ☑
Grand Master ☐

Tholothians have a distinctive scaled scalp with fleshy tendrils

JEDI FACT

Adi is also a skilled pilot. During the Clone Wars she pilots a red-and-white Delta-7B *Aethersprite*-class light interceptor

Lightsaber safely stored on belt

KEY FACTS

Homeworld:	Coruscant
Species:	Tholothian
Height:	1.84 m (6 ft)
Trained by:	Unknown
Appearances:	I, II, CW

RESCUE

When Adi is captured by the Separatist General Grievous, fellow Jedi Plo Koon organizes a rescue mission.

7

AHSOKA TANO

JEDI RANK

- [ ] Youngling
- [x] Padawan
- [ ] Knight
- [ ] Master
- [ ] Grand Master

Fearless, determined, and always ready to help anyone, Ahsoka Tano is everything a Jedi should be. However, she has decided to walk away from the Jedi Order and is finding her own ways to help bring peace to the galaxy.

PADAWAN

As a Padawan, Ahsoka is impulsive and brave—an ideal apprentice for Anakin Skywalker. Her experiences during the Clone Wars help her to mature and she learns to control her emotions.

JEDI FACT

Anakin nicknames Ahsoka "Snips" because of her sharp wit. In turn, she calls him "Skyguy." Although the pair grow close, the nicknames stick.

BETRAYAL

When Ahsoka's friend and fellow Padawan Barriss Offee bombs the Jedi Temple, she frames Ahsoka for the crime. Although Anakin discovers the true culprit, Ahsoka leaves the Jedi Order after this.

Hollow
montrals
sense
movement

KEY FACTS

Homeworld: Unknown
Species: Togruta
Height: 1.76 m (5 ft 9 in)
Trained by: Anakin Skywalker
Appearances: CW, R, M

Montrals
keep on
growing

Ahsoka's
Padawan
outfit

JEDI FACT

The Jedi Council sees
that Ahsoka is innocent,
but it is too late. She has
lost faith in the Jedi
Order and wants to
find a new path.

LIGHT SIDE

BRAVERY

WISDOM

LOYALTY

INNER STRENGTH

JUSTICE

WHO ARE THE SITH?

FALLEN JEDI

A few great Jedi have turned to the dark side. Some, like Count Dooku, lost faith in the Jedi Order, while others, such as Asajj Ventress, Anakin Skywalker, and Ben Solo could not control their emotions and were persuaded to turn to the dark side.

SITH

The dark side offers virtually unlimited power, but it is all-consuming. The Sith use anger, fear, and jealousy to get what they want, but they can never be happy. The dark side gradually corrupts an individual until little of their original personality remains.

JEDI

All Jedi are born with a natural ability to use the Force and they train for many years so that they can use their powers wisely. The Force connects Jedi to the world around them—they can feel things before they see them, move objects without touching them, react quickly to danger, and even sense whether someone is telling the truth.

The Sith are the enemies of the Jedi and their values are the complete opposite. The Force has two sides, a light side and a dark side. The Sith use the dark side of the Force to gain power and do not care about others, while the Jedi use the light side to live in harmony with the galaxy and to help others.

DARK SIDE

PASSION

FORBIDDEN KNOWLEDGE

GREED

SELFISHNESS

RAGE

JEDI RANK

- ☐ Youngling
- ☐ Padawan
- ☑ Knight
- ☐ Master
- ☐ Grand Master

ANAKIN SKYWALKER

Anakin Skywalker is one of the most famous and powerful Jedi ever. He is also one of the most troubled. As the Chosen One, he was supposed to bring balance to the Force, but Anakin's fears, frustrations, and deep love for his family led him down a darker path for many years.

EARLY LIFE

Anakin grows up enslaved on Tatooine, with his mother Shmi. He is a clever kid—he builds the droid C-3PO—and an expert pilot. As soon as Jedi Master Qui-Gon meets Anakin, he senses the boy is unusually strong with the Force.

GROWING UP

Anakin finds it hard to leave his mother, but forms a strong bond with Jedi Master Obi-Wan Kenobi. Anakin learns how to use his amazing Force powers, but he remains impulsive and reckless.

CHANGING SIDES

Anakin struggles to follow the Jedi Code and secretly marries Padmé Amidala. When he has visions of her death, he turns to the dark side to save her, making him an enemy of the Jedi.

Anakin is a Jedi hero, but he is also deeply troubled

Lightsaber is later used by his son Luke

Leather robes

KEY FACTS

Homeworld: Tatooine
Species: Human
Height: 1.85 m (6 ft 1 in)
Trained by: Obi-Wan Kenobi
Padawan: Ahsoka Tano
Appearances: I, II, CW, III, VI

JEDI RANK

- [ ] Youngling
- [ ] Padawan
- [ ] Knight
- [x] Master
- [ ] Grand Master

AGEN KOLAR

Agen Kolar's impulsive personality often sees him leap into battle without thinking. But he is highly skilled with a lightsaber and is confident he can defeat anyone.

JEDI FACT

Agen's lightsaber has dual crystals, which allow him to fight with either a blue or a green blade.

Jedi cloak

KEY FACTS

Homeworld:	Coruscant
Species:	Zabrak
Height:	1.9 m (6 ft 4 in)
Trained by:	Unknown
Padawan:	Tan Yuster
Appearances:	II, III

FINAL BATTLE

Even Agen's sword skills are no match for Darth Sidious. The Sith Lord defeats him and Kit Fisto with ease.

AVAR KRISS

Avar Kriss is a noble, selfless, and compassionate Jedi Master. Her Force powers are so strong that she can connect with multiple beings through the Force and share vital information.

JEDI RANK

Youngling ☐
Padawan ☐
Knight ☐
Master ☑
Grand Master ☐

IMPORTANT JOB

Avar takes command of the Starlight Beacon space station for a time. She proves herself to be a wise and caring leader.

KEY FACTS

Homeworld: Unknown
Species: Human
Height: 1.7 m (5 ft 8 in)
Trained by: Cheriff Maota
Appearances: THR

Jedi Temple attire

JEDI FACT

Following a terrible tragedy called the "Great Disaster," in which she saves many lives, Avar is known as the "Hero of Hetzal."

JEDI RANK

- [ ] Youngling
- [x] Padawan
- [ ] Knight
- [ ] Master
- [ ] Grand Master

BARRISS OFFEE

Barriss Offee is a hard-working and intelligent Padawan with a bright future ahead of her. However, during the Clone Wars Barriss loses faith in the Jedi Order and begins to believe that it is creating problems, not fixing them.

Mirialan face tattoos

JEDI FACT

Barriss turns her back on the Jedi Order. She attacks the Jedi Temple and then frames her friend Ahsoka for the crime.

KEY FACTS

Homeworld: Mirial
Species: Mirialan
Height: 1.66 m (5 ft 5 in)
Trained by: Luminara Unduli
Appearances: II, CW,

GREAT TEAM

Barriss is an expert in tandem fighting—she moves at exactly the same time as her master, Luminara Unduli.

BEN SOLO

Ben Solo has strong Force powers, just like his mother Leia and his uncle Luke. But, like his grandfather Anakin, he cannot resist the dark side. As the Sith Lord Kylo Ren, Ben tries to destroy the Jedi Order.

JEDI RANK

Youngling ☐
Padawan ☑
Knight ☐
Master ☐
Grand Master ☐

KEY FACTS

Homeworld: Chandrila
Species: Human
Height: 1.89 m (6 ft 2 in)
Trained by: Luke Skywalker
Appearances: VII, VIII, IX

Ben wears black, like his grandfather Darth Vader

JEDI FACT

Although he turns to the dark side for many years, Ben ultimately returns to the light side and becomes one with the Force.

FAMILY LOVE

When Ben finally turns back to the light side of the Force he finds peace. He realizes that his father, Han Solo, and his mother, Leia, have always loved him.

BULTAR SWAN

JEDI RANK

- ☐ Youngling
- ☐ Padawan
- ☑ Knight
- ☐ Master
- ☐ Grand Master

Jedi Knight Bultar Swan is selected by Mace Windu to help rescue Obi-Wan Kenobi and his Padawan. When the rescue mission becomes the Battle of Geonosis, Bultar's Jedi skills face the ultimate test.

IN ACTION

Bultar has been taught well by her Jedi Master. Although battle droids outnumber the Jedi, Bultar fights well and survives the First Battle of Geonosis.

Determined expression

JEDI FACT

During the Battle of Geonosis—the first battle of the Clone Wars—Bultar fights closely with fellow Jedi Stass Allie.

KEY FACTS

Homeworld:	Unknown
Species:	Human
Height:	1.68 m (5 ft 5 in)
Trained by:	Unknown
Appearances:	II

BURRYAGA

Although he is a Padawan, Burryaga is already extremely sensitive to the Force. He can detect things that more experienced Jedi cannot.

JEDI RANK

Youngling ☐
Padawan ☑
Knight ☐
Master ☐
Grand Master ☐

KEY FACTS

Homeworld: Kashyyyk
Species: Wookiee
Height: 2.23 m (7 ft 4 in)
Trained by: Nib Assek
Appearances: THR

JEDI FACT

Few non-Wookiees understand the Shyriiwook language, so Burryaga sometimes finds it hard to communicate.

Jedi Mission attire

SAVING OTHERS

During the Great Disaster, Burryaga is the only Jedi who knows people are in danger, hearing their calls through the Force. The gentle giant saves many lives that day.

BYPH

JEDI RANK

- ☑ Youngling
- ☐ Padawan
- ☐ Knight
- ☐ Master
- ☐ Grand Master

Byph is a talented youngling, but he sometimes struggles to overcome his fears. However, his good friends Petro, Katooni, Gungi, Ganodi, and Zatt are determined to help him.

❌ LIGHTSABER

Byph manages to face his fears and finds his kyber crystal. Building his own lightsaber will give him some much-needed confidence.

Ithorians have two mouths, one on each side of their necks

KEY FACTS

Homeworld: Ithor
Species: Ithorian
Height: 1.22 m (4 ft)
Trained by: Various
Appearances: CW

JEDI FACT

Like Byph, most Ithorians are peaceful and love nature. These are useful qualities for a Jedi.

CAL KESTIS

JEDI RANK

Youngling ☐
Padawan ☐
Knight ☑
Master ☐
Grand Master ☐

As a Padawan, Cal Kestis survives the purge that nearly wipes out the Jedi Order. He hides his true identity for many years, but is now determined to use his Force powers to help restore the Order.

NEW MISSION

Along with Cere Junda, Cal believes that the Jedi Order is the galaxy's best hope for overturning the Empire and restoring peace.

Cal does not wear Jedi robes

JEDI FACT

Cal's lightsaber is his third. It's double-bladed and the hilt can also be split to make two separate sabers.

KEY FACTS

Homeworld: Unknown
Species: Human
Height: 1.82 m (5 ft 9 in)
Trained by: Jaro Tapal, Cere Junda
Appearances: FO

WHERE DO YOU FIND KYBER CRYSTALS?

Kyber crystals occur naturally all over the galaxy, but the Jedi get theirs from the Crystal Cave on the ice planet of Ilum. Younglings use their Force powers to find their own special crystal.

WHAT IS A LIGHTSABER MADE OF?

The glowing blade of a lightsaber is made from a kyber energy crystal and the handle, known as a hilt, is made from metal and a variety of materials. Every Jedi makes their own lightsaber— it is an important stage of a youngling's training. Each lightsaber is unique, made to suit the size and combat style of the Jedi who will use it.

WHAT CAN A LIGHTSABER DO?

A lightsaber can cut through virtually anything, it can deflect blaster fire, and it can even be used as a torch!

DO ONLY JEDI HAVE LIGHTSABERS?

Only someone attuned to the Force can build a lightsaber—so that means the Sith too—but anyone can use one.

OBI-WAN KENOBI'S FIRST LIGHTSABER

Younglings practice with low-powered safety lightsabers so that they don't get injured.

QUI-GON JINN'S LIGHTSABER

DOES A JEDI ONLY HAVE ONE LIGHTSABER?

No. A Jedi can build more than one lightsaber. Anakin Skywalker loses his first lightsaber in the Battle of Geonosis and has to build a new one. That lightsaber is later used by Luke Skywalker, and then Rey. Some Jedi even use two lightsabers at once.

Jedi must build their lightsabers carefully. If the kyber crystal is not in the correct position, the lightsaber might explode.

YODA'S LIGHTSABER

ANAKIN SKYWALKER'S FIRST LIGHTSABER

MACE WINDU'S LIGHTSABER

DARTH SIDIOUS' LIGHTSABER

JEDI RANK

- ☐ Youngling
- ☐ Padawan
- ☑ Knight
- ☐ Master
- ☐ Grand master

CERE JUNDA

Cere Junda survives Order 66 and later escapes Darth Vader, but she is haunted by these experiences. She no longer considers herself a Jedi, but has faith in the Order and is determined to help restore it.

Wise but stern expression

KEY FACTS

Homeworld:	Unknown
Species:	Human
Height:	1.65 m (5 ft 4 in)
Trained by:	Eno Cordova
Padawans:	Trilla Suduri, Cal Kestis
Appearances:	FO

JEDI FACT

Before Order 66 was activated, Cere was a seeker—a Jedi that searched the galaxy for Force-sensitive younglings.

TEACHER

Cere senses Cal Kestis' Force powers and helps him to finish his training. In turn, Cal helps Cere to rebuild her own connection to the Force.

COLEMAN KCAJ

JEDI RANK 🪐

Coleman Kcaj's skills in meditation, diplomacy, strategy, and lightsaber combat make him a valued member of the Jedi Council. However, even he does not predict the rise of the Sith.

Youngling	☐
Padawan	☐
Knight	☐
Master	☑
Grand master	☐

KEY FACTS

Homeworld: Skustell
Species: Ongree
Height: 2.04 m (6 ft 8 in)
Trained by: Unknown
Appearances: III

JEDI FACT

Like all Ongree, Coleman has a distinctive face shape, with the narrowest part at the top and the eyes at the bottom.

Eyes are below mouth and nose

Traditional Jedi robes

SURVIVAL

Most of the Jedi Council did not survive Order 66, but it is believed that Coleman Kcaj did. His current whereabouts are unknown.

COLEMAN TREBOR

JEDI RANK

- ☐ Youngling
- ☐ Padawan
- ☐ Knight
- ☑ Master
- ☐ Grand Master

Coleman Trebor is the only Vurk to become a Jedi. He comes from the oceanic world of Sembla, and his species is famous for its empathy and calmness.

UNFAIR FIGHT

When Coleman battles the former Jedi Count Dooku he is sneakily shot by the Bounty Hunter Jango Fett.

JEDI FACT

Coleman's greatest skill is mediation. He is often able to settle disputes peacefully thanks to his calmness and wisdom.

Bony crest keeps growing throughout a Vurk's life

KEY FACTS

Homeworld: Sembla
Species: Vurk
Height: 2.13 m (7 ft)
Trained by: Unknown
Appearances: II

DEPA BILLABA

A wise and spiritual Jedi, Depa Billaba is a voice of reason on the Jedi Council. She is also an excellent teacher, telling her Padawan, Caleb Dume, that a Jedi must always be ready to sacrifice themself.

Chalacta Marks of Illumination

JEDI RANK

Youngling ☐
Padawan ☐
Knight ☐
Master ☑
Grand Master ☐

KEY FACTS

Homeworld: Chalacta
Species: Human
Height: 1.68 m (5 ft 6 in)
Trained by: Mace Windu
Padawan: Caleb Dume
Appearances: I, II, BB

JEDI FACT

Depa is a brave general during the Clone Wars. She is nearly killed by General Grievous but finds the strength to recover.

MASTER

Mace Windu rescued Depa from space pirates when she was a child. He then trained her as his Padawan.

27

DOOKU

Dooku was a respected Jedi Master, but he became dissatisfied with the Jedi Order and the Republic. He left the Order, later turning to the dark side and becoming a Sith.

NEW MASTER

Dooku now serves Darth Sidious. He craves power and wants to destroy the Jedi.

JEDI FACT

Dooku's lightsaber skills are more than a match for most Jedi, but he doesn't always fight fairly.

Cape reflects Dooku's status as Count of Serenno

KEY FACTS

Homeworld:	Serenno
Species:	Human
Height:	1.93 m (6 ft 4 in)
Trained by:	Yoda
Padawan:	Qui-Gon Jinn
Appearances:	II, CW, III

EVEN PIELL

Even Piell is one of the smallest Jedi, but also one of the Order's mightiest warriors. He lost an eye during a fight, but you can be sure he won the battle. Even's manner is gruff but he is an honorable Jedi.

DECISIONS

Even Piell also sits on the Jedi High Council. He votes against allowing Anakin Skywalker to begin his training.

Traditional Jedi topknot

KEY FACTS

Homeworld: Lannik
Species: Lannik
Height: 1.22 m (4 ft)
Trained by: Unknown
Appearances: I, II, CW

JEDI FACT

During the Clone Wars Even is taken prisoner. Wounded, he escapes and gives Ahsoka Tano vital information.

EZRA BRIDGER

JEDI RANK

- ☐ Youngling
- ☑ Padawan
- ☐ Knight
- ☐ Master
- ☐ Grand Master

Ezra Bridger is a young orphan with Force powers. He lives aboard the starship *Ghost* with a group of other rebels who oppose the evil Galactic Empire in its early days.

JEDI FACT

Ezra has the potential to become a powerful Jedi Knight, but he must be cautious as he is also drawn to the dark side.

Ezra is learning how to use a jet pack

Helmet

KEY FACTS

Homeworld: Lothal
Species: Human
Height: 1.65 m (5 ft 5 in)
Trained by: Kanan Jarrus
Appearances: R

JEDI SKILLS

Ezra trains hard with Kanan Jarrus. He also has several chances to practice his lightsaber skills for real.

GANODI

Youngling ☑
Padawan ☐
Knight ☐
Master ☐
Grand Master ☐

As a youngling, Ganodi still has a lot to learn about being a Jedi. Few Rodians have ever become Jedi and Ganodi is determined to do well in her training at the Jedi Temple on Coruscant.

FRIENDS

Ganodi and her friends Katooni and Gungi help each other when they have to go on real missions, such as rescuing Ahsoka from pirates.

Typical Rodian spiny crest

JEDI FACT

Ganodi struggles to find the right crystal to make her lightsaber. There are so many! But she uses the Force to guide her.

Rodians are cold-blooded and have scaly skin

KEY FACTS

Homeworld: Rodia
Species: Rodian
Height: 1.19 m (3 ft 11 in)
Trained by: Various
Appearances: CW

31

JEDI RANK

- ☑ Youngling
- ☐ Padawan
- ☐ Knight
- ☐ Master
- ☐ Grand Master

Grogu is the same species as Yoda and Yaddle—but no one knows what that species is called. He has the potential to become a legendary Jedi, but his life is in constant danger.

Large, pointed green ears

JEDI FACT

Grogu is only a little bigger than a football, but he is so strong with the Force that he can lift a giant mudhorn!

KEY FACTS

Homeworld:	Unknown
Species:	Unknown
Height:	34 cm (1 ft 1 in)
Trained by:	Various
Appearances:	M

"THE CHILD"

Grogu is 50 years old, but that's young for his species! He acts a little like a human toddler and loves food.

GUNGI

Gungi is a promising young Jedi. Most Wookiees are fierce warriors led by their emotions, so few are chosen to be Jedi. Gungi is learning how to be calm and patient, like a true Jedi.

TRAINING IN ACTION

When locating the special crystal for his lightsaber, Gungi has to be patient. He must wait for water to freeze over before he can cross the ice and grab his crystal.

Gungi made a wooden hilt for his lightsaber

Thick, shaggy hair

JEDI FACT

Gungi may grow to be up to 3 meters tall (9 ft 10 in). But as a Jedi, he will learn from Master Yoda that "size matters not."

KEY FACTS

Homeworld: Kashyyyk
Species: Wookiee
Height: 1.53 m (5 ft)
Trained by: Various
Appearances: CW

WHAT TRAINING DOES A JEDI NEED?

Not everyone has what it takes to be a Jedi. First of all, a being needs to be sensitive to the Force. Most Jedi recruits reveal their Force abilities when they are very young and many begin their training as babies. Jedi can come from anywhere in the galaxy, and it takes most individuals more than 20 years to complete their training.

1

YOUNGLING

Force-sensitive children leave their families to go and live at the Jedi Temple on Coruscant. Known as younglings, they study the Force, learn to control their Force abilities, and begin lightsaber training.

2

PADAWAN

When a youngling is ready, they become an apprentice (Padawan) to a Jedi Knight or Jedi Master. They receive intensive, one-to-one training in the Force and lightsaber combat, and may go on some missions.

JEDI KNIGHT

3

To become a Knight, a Padawan must pass the Jedi Trials. The Trials have nine aspects—teamwork, isolation, fear, anger, betrayal, focus, instinct, forgiveness, and protection—and can be set by their master, or occur on a mission.

JEDI FACT

Most younglings are discovered by other Jedi. A painless blood test checks their midi-chlorian count to confirm the child's Jedi potential.

JEDI MASTER

4

Not all Knights become Jedi Masters; this honor can only be given by the Grand Master, when they believe a Jedi is worthy. Jedi Masters or Knights may train Padawans, but only Jedi Masters may join the Jedi High Council.

GRAND MASTER

5

The Grand Master is the leader of the whole Jedi Order, so there can only be one at a time. Yoda's wisdom, experience, and patience make him an ideal Grand Master. He listens and meditates, working closely with the Jedi Council to make decisions.

JEDI OF THE HIGH REPUBLIC

The Jedi Order has been protecting the galaxy for thousands of years. It has faced many challenges and seen many shifts in power. However, the era known as the High Republic was one of the most exciting periods for the galaxy, and during this time, the Jedi Order flourished. Let's meet a few more of its distinguished members.

STELLAN GIOS

Calm, reasonable, and optimistic, Jedi Master Stellan Gios works well with more impulsive Jedi. He also enjoys teaming up with his old friend Avar Kriss. Stellan is a natural teacher. His Padawan, Vernestra Rwoh, becomes a Jedi Knight at only fifteen, although this is due to her talents as much as his guidance!

SSKEER

This Trandoshan Jedi Master is known for his strong opinions. He lost an arm and a friend in battle, which has affected his connection to the Force. As a result of those losses, Sskeer has been tempted to turn to the dark side, but he has resisted.

BELL ZETTIFAR

Bell Zettifar is a detemined Padawan who was once trained by Master Loden Greatstorm, and who is now trained by Master Indeera Stokes. Bell saves many lives when the Republic Fair is attacked by Nihil marauders.

KEEVE TRENNIS

Newly promoted Knight Keeve Trennis, who was trained by Master Sskeer, is a talented and quick-thinking Jedi with a great future ahead of her. She has already distinguished herself in battle against the Drengir, a carnivorous plant-like species.

JOCASTA NU

Jocasta Nu is the Chief Librarian of the Jedi Archives, which are located in the Jedi Temple on Coruscant. The Archives are believed to contain all the knowledge in the galaxy.

Neat bun hairstyle

MISSING PLANET

Jocasta has total faith in the Archives and is not happy when Obi-Wan Kenobi suggests that the planet Kamino is somehow missing.

KEY FACTS

Homeworld: Coruscant
Species: Human
Height: 1.69 m (5 ft 7 in)
Trained by: Unknown
Appearances: II, CW

JEDI FACT

She doesn't use her combat skills much in her current job, but Jocasta is a Jedi Master and has undergone full Jedi training.

Comfortable and elegant robes

KANAN JARRUS

Padawan Caleb Dume survived Order 66, thanks to his brave Jedi Master, Depa Billaba. He was forced into hiding to save his life and changed his name to Kanan Jarrus. For a time, Kanan gave up being a Jedi completely.

Shoulder armor

KEY FACTS

Homeworld: Coruscant
Species: Human
Height: 1.91 m (6 ft 3 in)
Trained by: Depa Billaba
Padawan: Ezra Bridger
Appearances: CW, BB, R

JEDI FACT

When he was a child at the Jedi Temple Kanan met many famous Jedi, such as Luminara Unduli and even Master Yoda.

Kanan did not complete his own lightsaber training

FORCE LESSONS

Although officially only a Padawan, Kanan trains Ezra Bridger in the ways of the Force. He sees it as his Jedi duty to help the boy learn how to control his powers.

KATOONI

Although she's still a youngling, Katooni already possesses many core Jedi skills. She is patient, kind, and not afraid to stand up for what she believes in.

JEDI FACT

Katooni is not a big fan of heights. However, she has to overcome her fear to reach the crystal for her lightsaber.

Katooni took great care in building her lightsaber

She is still learning how to fight with a lightsaber

KEY FACTS

Homeworld:	Tholoth
Species:	Tholothian
Height:	1.3 m (4 ft 3 in)
Trained by:	Various
Appearances:	CW

DIPLOMAT

When the younglings encounter the pirate Hondo Ohnaka, Katooni persuades him to help them.

KI-ADI-MUNDI

Youngling ☐
Padawan ☐
Knight ☐
Master ☑
Grand Master ☐

Ki-Adi-Mundi is wise and logical. His large brain allows him to see all sides of a situation, but it also means that he struggles to accept "impossible" ideas—such as the return of the Sith.

Large, domed head

KEY FACTS

Homeworld: Cerea
Species: Cerean
Height: 1.98 m (6 ft 6 in)
Trained by: Yoda
Appearances: I, II, CW, III

JEDI FACT

Ki-Adi-Mundi is not just wise, he is also an agile fighter with superfast reflexes.

Defensive stance

TREACHERY

Although he is a skilled warrior, Ki-Adi-Mundi has no chance against his clone troopers when Order 66 is activated.

KIT FISTO

Amphibious Kit Fisto can breathe in air or water, so he is skilled in both land and underwater combat. He can also use his Force powers to manipulate water.

⊗ INTO BATTLE

Kit is able to fight many opponents at one time. These combat skills help him to survive the Battle of Geonosis.

Sensitive eyes

Amphibious tentacles

JEDI FACT

Kit's head tentacles are extremely sensitive and allow him to read others' emotions. It's a useful skill, especially in battle.

KEY FACTS

Homeworld:	Glee Anselm
Species:	Nautolan
Height:	1.96 m (6 ft 5 in)
Trained by:	Unknown
Padawan:	Nahdar Vebb
Appearances:	II, CW, III

LUMINARA UNDULI

Luminara Unduli is famous for her wisdom and calmness. She teaches her Padawan, Barriss Offee, to prepare well for her missions and to remember that others' lives depend on their choices.

JEDI RANK

Youngling ☐
Padawan ☐
Knight ☐
Master ☑
Grand Master ☐

Traditional Mirialan headdress

Bracelets are from Mirial

JEDI FACT

Kanan Jarrus and Ezra Bridger hear rumors that Luminara survived the Jedi Purge. She did not, it is just a cruel trick by the Empire.

KEY FACTS

Homeworld: Mirial
Species: Mirialan
Height: 1.76 m (5 ft 9 in)
Trained by: Unknown
Padawan: Barriss Offee
Appearances: II, CW, III, R

FIERCE FIGHTER

Luminara is a skilled fighter, both with and without a lightsaber. She fights well in the epic Battle of Geonosis and later survives a duel with the deadly Asajj Ventress.

43

- ☐ Youngling
- ☑ Padawan
- ☐ Knight
- ☐ Master
- ☐ Grand Master

LEIA ORGANA

Princess, diplomat, rebel, general, and Jedi—Leia has many different roles. She is a strong and brave leader, who is always willing to stand up for what she believes in, no matter what it takes.

Regal, braided hairstyle

JEDI FACT

Leia is an adult before she learns that she is really the daughter of Anakin Skywalker and Padmé Amidala and that she has a twin brother—Luke.

Serious expression

Leia has never worn Jedi robes

MISSING PIECE

Leia has always had strong instincts about events and people. When Luke tells her that they are twins, she finally understands that she has been feeling the Force.

FAMILY

After the Battle of Endor, Leia marries the smuggler-turned-hero Han Solo. Their son Ben is strong with the Force, but he succumbs to the dark side, just like his grandfather Anakin.

KEY FACTS

Homeworld: Alderaan
Species: Human
Height: 1.55 m (5 ft 1 in)
Trained by: Luke Skywalker
Padawan: Rey
Appearances: III, R, RO, IV, V, VI, VII, VIII, IX

JEDI FACT

Like most Jedi, Leia is able to sense others through the Force, especially Luke. And thanks to him, she is also skilled with a lightsaber.

REBEL LEADER

Over the years, Leia has learned to be a brilliant military strategist. She realizes, though, that the best leaders put protecting others above defeating their enemies.

🌀 JEDI RANK

- ☐ Youngling
- ☐ Padawan
- ☐ Knight
- ☑ Master
- ☐ Grand Master

TRUE PATH

Luke's life changes when he discovers a message inside the droid R2-D2. It leads him to the Rebel Alliance, where his skills as a pilot help to save the galaxy.

JEDI FACT

When Luke senses Grogu through the Force, he travels to find him. He promises to train him as a Jedi and to protect him.

Warm cloak

Traditional Jedi robes

KEY FACTS

Homeworld:	Tatooine
Species:	Human
Height:	1.72 m (5 ft 8 in)
Trained by:	Yoda
Padawans:	Ben Solo, Rey
Appearances:	III, IV, V, VI, M, VII, VIII, IX

LUKE SKYWALKER

As a young man, Luke was impulsive and desperate for adventure, but after many years of study, he has become a wise and patient Jedi Master. He understands his responsibilities as a Jedi and will always help anyone who needs him.

JEDI TRAINING

Although Luke is much older than most Padawans, he is trained by Grand Master Yoda. Later, when Luke becomes a Jedi Master, he trains his sister Leia, his nephew Ben, and Rey, as well as many other young Jedi.

ULTIMATE BATTLE

Luke is tempted to join the dark side when Darth Vader reveals that he is Luke's father. Luke resists, and instead his strong Jedi values help to redeem Vader. It brings peace and hope to the galaxy, for a short time at least.

JEDI FACT

Luke feels an instant connection with Princess Leia. When he learns that he has a twin sister, he senses immediately that it is Leia.

WHAT POWERS DO JEDI HAVE?

Jedi are born with a connection to the Force, but they spend years training their powers. They learn to use their abilities wisely, for defense not attack, and to preserve peace, not to make war. In the wrong hands, the Force can be deadly...

JEDI MIND TRICK

With a wave of the hand, a Jedi can make you do what they want or forget what you have seen. Obi-Wan makes it look easy, but it takes practice—it took Rey several attempts to trick a stormtrooper.

TELEKINESIS

Wouldn't it be great to be able to move objects without even touching them? Anakin uses this power to impress Padmé, while Yoda uses it to defend himself against the former Jedi Count Dooku. A Jedi can also use the Force to summon their lightsaber instantly.

AGILITY

Jedi can't fly but they are super agile. They can usually react quicker, move faster, and jump further than their enemies. Their knowledge of the Force also gives them fast reactions.

VISIONS

Those who are sensitive to the Force can experience visions (a bit like dreams) of the past, present, or future. Rey sees herself as a Sith, and she knows she must stop this vision from coming true.

ACUTE SENSE

Those who don't know they're a Jedi might dismiss this power as intuition or instinct, but it's so much more than that. Force users can sense each others' presence and feelings. Leia hears Luke when he calls out to her using the Force.

FORCE SPIRIT

When Jedi die, they become one with the Force. However, some Jedi have the ability to retain their bodies in spirit form and can communicate with the living.

DYAD

In very rare cases, two can become one with the Force. Rey and Kylo Ren are a dyad—able to communicate with each other and feel each other's thoughts.

SITH POWERS

The Jedi use the light side of the Force, but there are many powers on the dark side, too. These powers are designed to hurt or kill. Here, Dooku uses Force-generated lightning to try and defeat Yoda.

JEDI RANK

- ☐ Youngling
- ☐ Padawan
- ☐ Knight
- ☑ Master
- ☐ Grand Master

MACE WINDU

Mace Windu will do whatever he thinks is necessary to protect the Jedi Order. Whether that's disagreeing with the rest of the Jedi Council, or risking his own life, his duty as a Jedi is his top priority.

Ready for action

Distinctive purple lightsaber

Jedi battle outfit

JEDI WISDOM

When Qui-Gon Jinn asks the Jedi Council for permission to train Anakin Skywalker, Mace does not think it's a good idea. He senses danger, as well as potential, in the young boy.

OUTNUMBERED

Mace acts quickly when he needs to. He assembles a Jedi task force to go to Geonosis and rescue Obi-Wan, Anakin, and Padmé. When the battle becomes a war, Mace is ready.

KEY FACTS

Homeworld: Haruun Kal
Species: Human
Height: 1.88 m (6 ft 2 in)
Trained by: Cyslin Myr, Yoda
Padawan: Depa Billaba
Appearances: I, II, CW, III

JEDI FACT

When Anakin is allowed to become a Padawan, Mace remains suspicious of him, although he respects his achievements during the Clone Wars.

FACING THE SITH

When Chancellor Palpatine is revealed to be the Sith Lord Darth Sidious, Mace confronts him with an elite Jedi team. All are defeated, with Anakin joining Sidious against Mace.

- ☐ Youngling
- ☐ Padawan
- ☑ Knight
- ☐ Master
- ☐ Grand Master

NAHDAR VEBB

Like many young Jedi, Nahdar Vebb has to finish his training early to fight in the Clone Wars. Nahdar feels that he is ready to be a leader, but he lacks patience as well as experience.

The single barbel on Nahdar's chin is a sign of his youth

KEY FACTS

Homeworld: Mon Cala
Species: Mon Calamari
Height: 1.86 m (6 ft 1 in)
Trained by: Kit Fisto
Appearances: CW

Webbed hands

JEDI FACT

During the Clone Wars, Nahdar shows that he is a gifted Force healer. He helps wounded members of the Republic army.

✗ RUSHING IN

During a confrontation with the Separatist General Grievous, Kit Fisto advises caution. But Vebb's inexperience is his downfall.

OPPO RANCISIS

JEDI RANK ⚜

Youngling ☐
Padawan ☐
Knight ☐
Master ☑
Grand Master ☐

Oppo Rancisis is a wise Jedi Master who has sat on the Jedi Council since the days of the High Republic. He does not make decisions lightly, considering all sides of an issue before taking action.

SENSING DANGER

When Qui-Gon Jinn asks permission to train young Anakin Skywalker, Oppo sees that doing so could threaten the safety of the Jedi Order.

Oppo has four arms—two are hidden in his robes

KEY FACTS

Homeworld: Thisspias
Species: Thisspiasian
Height: 1.38 m (4 ft 6 in) when coiled
Trained by: Yaddle
Padawan: Dal
Appearances: THR, II, CW

Snakelike tail

JEDI FACT

In battle, Oppo prefers using his Force powers instead of his lightsaber. His tail makes a useful weapon, too!

OBI-WAN KENOBI

Obi-Wan Kenobi always thinks before leaping into action. He is wise, patient, and loyal to the Jedi Code. However, he is also a skilled fighter and will make difficult choices—and even break the rules—if he believes that it's the right thing to do.

JEDI FACT

Obi-Wan is a skilled pilot, but he dislikes flying due to a bad experience with the "autopursuit" function on a starfighter when he was younger.

Defensive stance

Emergency food capsules kept here

Clip for lightsaber

KEY FACTS

Homeworld: Stewjon
Species: Human
Height: 1.79 m (5 ft 10 in)
Trained by: Qui-Gon Jinn
Padawan: Anakin Skywalker
Appearances: I, II, CW, III, R, IV, V, VI

FAST LEARNER

As a Padawan, Obi-Wan learns how to be resourceful, compassionate, and wise from Qui-Gon. Obi-Wan becomes a Jedi Knight after defeating the Sith Darth Maul. To honor his master's dying wish, he takes Anakin Skywalker as his Padawan.

GREAT TEAM

Obi-Wan forms a strong bond with Anakin and hopes to guide him toward becoming a great Jedi. Both Obi-Wan and Anakin fight bravely in the Clone Wars, but Obi-Wan senses that Anakin is growing frustrated and confused.

NOBLE JEDI

Obi-Wan can't stop Anakin from turning to the dark side, but he can protect Anakin's children. He hides Luke and Leia so that their father has no idea that they even exist. Years later, Obi-Wan faces his old Padawan and sacrifices his own life to save Luke Skywalker.

JEDI FACT

After the Jedi Purge, Obi-Wan goes into hiding on Tatooine. From there, he can also watch over young Luke Skywalker.

- ☐ Youngling
- ☐ Padawan
- ☑ Knight
- ☐ Master
- ☐ Grand Master

PABLO-JILL

Like many Jedi, Pablo-Jill is part of the mission to rescue Obi-Wan, Anakin, and Padmé Amidala. When that turns into the First Battle of Geonosis, he fights bravely with his fellow Jedi.

Mouth has no lips

KEY FACTS

Homeworld: Skustell
Species: Ongree
Height: 2.04 m (6 ft 8 in)
Trained by: Unknown
Appearances: II

JEDI FACT

During the Clone Wars, Pablo-Jill's lightsaber is stolen by the Separatist cyborg General Grievous.

Robes cover multi-jointed legs

UPSIDE DOWN

Pablo-Jill's features are in the opposite order to humans, with a chin-like point at the top, followed by a mouth, four nostrils, and stalklike eyes.

PETRO

Quick-thinking and confident,
Petro is one of the most talented
younglings at the Jedi Temple.
However, he can be impatient
and impulsive, prioritizing
speed and action over honoring
Jedi traditions.

✕ CLEVER IDEA

Petro uses his Force
powers to join the
circus as part of a
mission to rescue
Ahsoka Tano.

JEDI FACT

Petro does not listen to
Professor Huyang when
he builds his lightsaber,
and has to start all
over again.

Ready
for
action

KEY FACTS

Homeworld: Corellia
Species: Human
Height: 1.26 m (4 ft 2 in)
Trained by: Various
Appearances: CW

JEDI RANK

- ☐ Youngling
- ☐ Padawan
- ☐ Knight
- ☑ Master
- ☐ Grand Master

PLO KOON

Calm and rational, Plo Koon is a respected member of the Jedi Council. He is known for his patience and skill as a pilot. During the Clone Wars, he acts as a mentor to Ahsoka Tano.

Mask protects him from oxygen, which is poisonous for Kel Dor

KEY FACTS

Homeworld:	Dorin
Species:	Kel Dor
Height:	1.88 m (6 ft 2 in)
Trained by:	Unknown
Padawan:	Unknown
Appearances:	I, II, CW, III

JEDI FACT

Plo Koon discovered Ahsoka Tano as an infant and brought her to Coruscant to begin her Jedi training.

PILOT

Although Plo is one of the best Jedi pilots, he does not stand a chance when Order 66 is activated and his ship is shot down by clone troopers.

QUINLAN VOS

JEDI RANK

Youngling ☐
Padawan ☐
Knight ☐
Master ☑
Grand Master ☐

Quinlan Vos doesn't dress like other Jedi and he doesn't always follow the rules. However, he has a special ability—when he touches objects, he can access the memories of anyone else who has handled them.

Face tattoos show Quinlan's clan

JEDI FACT

Quinlan Vos turns to the dark side and becomes Count Dooku's apprentice. But he finds his way back to the light side again.

Armor is not usually worn by Jedi

KEY FACTS

Homeworld: Kiffu
Species: Kiffar
Height: 1.91 m (6 ft 3 in)
Trained by: Unknown
Padawan: Aayla Secura
Appearances: I, CW

TEAMING UP

Quinlan is not a natural team player, but he works with Obi-Wan Kenobi to find Ziro the Hutt, and with the former assassin Asajj Ventress to find Darth Sidious.

QUI-GON JINN

Qui-Gon Jinn wants to bring balance to the galaxy, but has his own ideas about how to do that. He respects Jedi traditions, but is not afraid to break the Jedi Code or to go against the Jedi Council if he thinks it's the right thing to do.

UNUSUAL MASTER

Qui-Gon and his Padawan Obi-Wan Kenobi have different ideas about how to be a Jedi. Nevertheless, they trust each other—and Obi-Wan has to admit that his unconventional teacher is often right.

JEDI FACT

Qui-Gon confirms his beliefs about Anakin by testing the boy's midi-chlorian level. Anakin's is over 20,000—higher than any known Jedi.

KEY FACTS

Homeworld: Coruscant
Species: Human
Height: 1.93 m (6 ft 4 in)
Trained by: Dooku
Padawan: Obi-Wan Kenobi
Appearances: I, CW

CHOSEN ONE

He dislikes rules, but Qui-Gon believes in prophecies. He is sure that Anakin Skywalker is the Chosen One—the individual who will restore balance to the Force. He is determined to train him as a Jedi.

JEDI FACT

The Jedi believed that the Sith had been defeated. But, when Darth Maul confronts Qui-Gon on Tatooine, it is revealed that the Sith have simply been hiding.

Hair worn longer than most Jedi

Qui-Gon will do what he thinks is right

Jedi cloak worn for traveling

⊗ FINAL WISH

Qui-Gon duels the Sith Lord Darth Maul twice. The first time the Jedi cleverly escapes, but the second time he is killed by the brutal Sith. Before he dies, Qui-Gon makes Obi-Wan promise to train Anakin.

JEDI RANK

☐ Youngling
☐ Padawan
☐ Knight
☑ Master
☐ Grand Master

JEDI FACT

When Rey battles her grandfather, she is helped by the spirits of all the Jedi that have ever lived.

TOUGH LIFE

Rey grows up alone on the desert planet Jakku and survives by scavenging. She is tough and strong, but always willing to help others, such as the droid BB-8 and former stormtrooper Finn.

BEING A JEDI

Rey's Force powers reveal themselves when she touches the Skywalker lightsaber. At first Rey does not want to be a Jedi, but eventually she asks Luke Skywalker to train her.

SPECIAL BOND

Rey can't understand the connection she has with the First Order's Kylo Ren—he is her enemy. Rey learns that it is the Force that links them and helps Kylo Ren to find his way back to the light side.

REY

Although her grandfather is Emperor Palpatine, Rey rejects the dark side and honors the Jedi traditions she learns from Luke and Leia. Rey is strong with the Force and is determined to bring peace and hope to the galaxy again.

Rey focuses her mind

Lightsaber once belonged to Anakin and Luke Skywalker

Belt known as an obi

KEY FACTS

Homeworld: Jakku
Species: Human
Height: 1.7 m (5 ft 7 in)
Trained by: Leia Organa, Luke Skywalker
Appearances: VII, VIII, IX

- ☐ Youngling
- ☐ Padawan
- ☐ Knight
- ☑ Master
- ☐ Grand Master

SAESEE TIIN

Saesee Tiin is a Jedi of few words. He prefers to let his actions do the talking, showing great courage and skill in battle. Saesee is an expert with a lightsaber and an excellent pilot.

Large horns and strong forehead can be used as a weapon

KEY FACTS

Homeworld: Iktotch
Species: Iktotchi
Height: 1.88 m (6 ft 2 in)
Trained by: Unknown
Appearances: I, II, CW, III

JEDI FACT

Saesee has highly developed telepathic skills, even for a Jedi. This means he can speak to others via thoughts.

JEDI HONOR

After the death of Qui-Gon Jinn, Saesee and the rest of the Jedi Council agree to let Anakin train as a Jedi.

SHAAK TI

JEDI RANK

Youngling ☐
Padawan ☐
Knight ☐
Master ☑
Grand Master ☐

Shaak Ti has an important job during the Clone Wars: overseeing the training of the clone troopers on Kamino. Wise and patient, she treats the clones with respect and compassion. She also senses the growing threat of the Sith.

Hollow horns known as montrals

KEY FACTS

Homeworld: Shili
Species: Togruta
Height: 1.78 m (5 ft 10 in)
Trained by: Unknown
Appearances: II, CW, III

JEDI FACT

Shaak Ti is proud to be a Togruta and a Jedi. She wears a traditional Togruta dress underneath her Jedi robes.

EXTRA SENSE

Shaak Ti's hollow montrals help her to sense any movement around her, giving her an advantage during battle.

65

SIFO-DYAS

Sifo-Dyas thinks that the galaxy is heading for war and that the Jedi Order should build an army. The Jedi Council does not agree, so Sifo-Dyas takes matters into his own hands.

A younger Sifo-Dyas—he was actually around 70 when he died

JEDI FACT

As a youngling, Sifo-Dyas was good friends with another trainee Jedi, Dooku. Later, their lives took different paths.

SECRET PLAN

Sifo-Dyas secretly orders a clone army to be prepared on Kamino. It is eventually discovered by Obi-Wan Kenobi, 10 years after Sifo-Dyas' death.

A hologram of Sifo-Dyas exists in the Jedi Archives

KEY FACTS

Homeworld: Minashee
Species: Human
Height: 1.8 m (5 ft 11 in)
Trained by: Lene Kostana
Appearances: CW

STASS ALLIE

Stass Allie fights bravely alongside her fellow Jedi during the Battle of Geonosis and the Clone Wars, but her greatest skill is her Force healing power.

JEDI FACT

Stass is the cousin of Adi Gallia. After Gallia's death in the Clone Wars, Stass takes her place on the Jedi Council.

Tholoth tendrils

Short battle robes

KEY FACTS

Homeworld: Tholoth
Species: Tholothian
Height: 1.8 m (5 ft 11 in)
Trained by: Unknown
Appearances: II, III

DIPLOMATIC AIDE

Along with Plo Koon, Stass works closely with Senator Palpatine during the final years of the Galactic Republic. She has no idea who he really is...

WHO IS THE GREATEST JEDI EVER?

What makes a great Jedi? Extraordinary Force abilities? Great adventures and famous battles? Superb lightsaber skills? Legendary wisdom? All the Jedi here could lay claim to the honor of being the greatest-ever Jedi, but does one of them have the edge? Let's examine the case for each of them.

THE PROTECTOR

Obi-Wan defeats Darth Maul and Anakin Skywalker, he successfully hides Anakin's children, and when he dies, he becomes a Force spirit. Great, yes, but not quite the greatest.

THE CHOSEN ONE

Anakin Skywalker's midi-chlorian level is remarkable and his Jedi powers are exceptional. Although he turns to the dark side, he eventually returns to the light side, bringing balance to the Force, and fulfilling his destiny as the Chosen One. One of the greatest for sure, but there is another...

THE LEGEND

As the Jedi Grand Master, few creatures in the galaxy have not heard of Yoda or his legendary wisdom. He's also a fierce warrior and wonderful teacher. But one greater than Yoda there may be...

THE LAST JEDI

First Luke Skywalker brought hope to the galaxy, then for many years he was the last Jedi. Although he has saved the galaxy more than once, maybe Luke is not quite the greatest.

GREAT SACRIFICE

Born into a famous Jedi family, Ben Solo had enormous potential. Although he strayed from the Jedi path , sacrificing his life to save Rey is an act of true greatness.

A NEW JEDI

Although her grandfather, Emperor Palpatine, calls her to the dark side, Rey is able to resist. Her sensitivity to the Force allows her to draw strength from all the Jedi that have gone before her to finally defeat the Sith. Embodying the wisdom and courage of all the Jedi, Rey is potentially the greatest Jedi ever. So far...

JEDI RANK

- ☐ Youngling
- ☐ Padawan
- ☑ Knight
- ☐ Master
- ☐ Grand Master

TIPLAR

Like all Mikkians, Tiplar values honesty and honor above everything. She is a brave and loyal Jedi and becomes a general during the Clone Wars.

Head-tendrils detect sounds as most Mikkians have no ears

JEDI FACT

Tiplar is killed when a clone trooper malfunctions and carries out Order 66 early.

Face tattoo is identical to Tiplee's

KEY FACTS

Homeworld: Mikkia
Species: Mikkian
Height: 1.8 m (5 ft 11 in)
Trained by: Unknown
Appearances: CW

TWIN POWER

Tiplar works best alongside her twin sister Tiplee. They are both formidable and determined warriors.

TIPLEE

JEDI RANK ⓙ

Youngling ☐
Padawan ☐
Knight ☑
Master ☐
Grand Master ☐

Just like her twin, Tiplee is a noble and courageous Jedi Knight. As a Jedi general she fights bravely in the Clone Wars alongside her sister Tiplar, Anakin Skywalker, and Obi-Wan Kenobi.

MYSTERY

After her twin's death, Tiplee and Anakin question CT-5385, known as "Tup," the clone trooper responsible. But he can't remember his actions.

JEDI FACT

Shortly after her sister's death, Tiplee is killed during a duel with Count Dooku.

Head-tendrils can also detect temperature and radiation

Same style robes as her twin

KEY FACTS

Homeworld: Mikkia
Species: Mikkian
Height: 1.79 m (5 ft 10 in)
Trained by: Unknown
Appearances: CW

YADDLE

Yaddle is a wise Jedi scholar and spends a lot of time studying the Jedi Archives. However, she is also patient, kind, and always ready to help or advise her fellow Jedi.

KEY FACTS

Homeworld:	Unknown
Species:	Unknown
Height:	61 cm (2 ft)
Padawan:	Oppo Rancisis
Appearances:	1

JEDI FACT

Yaddle is the same species as Yoda, but she's much younger. At only 477 years old, she's around half Yoda's age.

Jedi Council seat is just the right size for Yaddle

Yaddle is a great listener

QUIET LIFE

After the Battle of Naboo, Yaddle decides to step down from the Jedi Council. Her place is taken by Shaak Ti.

YARAEL POOF

JEDI RANK ⨀

Youngling ☐
Padawan ☐
Knight ☐
Master ☑
Grand Master ☐

An expert in Jedi mind tricks, Yarael Poof mostly uses his skills to solve conflicts—and sometimes to play pranks on his fellow Jedi. His spineless body allows Yarael to perform incredible moves with a lightsaber.

JEDI LEADER

Yarael has sat on the Jedi Council since the days of the High Republic. After his death, he is replaced on the Council by Coleman Trebor.

KEY FACTS

Homeworld: Quermia
Species: Quermian
Height: 2.64 m (8 ft 8 in)
Trained by: Unknown
Appearances: THR, I

Quermians have long necks but no spines

Robes conceal a second set of arms

JEDI FACT

Like all Quermians, Yarael has a second brain located in his chest. He also has no nose, and senses smell through his fingers.

YODA

JEDI RANK

- ☐ Youngling
- ☐ Padawan
- ☐ Knight
- ☐ Master
- ☑ Grand Master

During his 900 years, Yoda has trained many Jedi and visited most parts of the galaxy. His wisdom is legendary. As Grand Master, Yoda has led the Jedi Council, and the entire Jedi Order, since the days of the High Republic.

JEDI FACT

No one knows where Yoda comes from, what species he is, or even who trained him. Something of a mystery he is.

Yoda's sensitive ears move to express his feelings

KEY FACTS

Homeworld:	Unknown
Species:	Unknown
Height:	66 cm (2 ft 2 in)
Trained by:	Unknown
Padawans:	Kantam Sy, Lula Talisola, Dooku, Cin Drallig, Mace Windu, Ki-Adi-Mundi, Luke Skywalker
Appearances:	THR, I, II, CW, III, R, V, IV, VIII

JEDI FACT

Yoda has a great sense of humor. He enjoys teasing Luke when his prospective pupil doesn't realize that Yoda is the legendary Jedi he is looking for.

❌ MASTER DUELIST

When battle is the only option, Yoda is an expert fighter. He is agile, skilled with a lightsaber, and has awesome Force abilities. When Yoda duels Count Dooku, his old Padawan flees to save himself.

TEACHING STYLE

Yoda is a patient teacher and prefers to let his apprentices work things out for themselves. Many find this frustrating, but Yoda teaches his students to be focused and objective, and to find answers from within.

IN EXILE

Although Yoda senses some disturbances in the Force, he does not predict the rise of the Sith. After the Jedi Purge, a sad Yoda goes into hiding on the remote planet Dagobah. Years later, Luke Skywalker restores hope to Yoda, and to the galaxy.

JEDI RANK

- ☑ Youngling
- ☐ Padawan
- ☐ Knight
- ☐ Master
- ☐ Grand Master

Zatt is a talented youngling who loves technology and science. However, sometimes, he needs to rely on his Force instincts to guide him, instead of gadgets.

Tendrils help Nautolans to read others' emotions

KEY FACTS

Homeworld: Glee Anselm
Species: Nautolan
Height: 1.21 m (4 ft)
Trained by: Various
Appearances: CW

Ready for action

JEDI FACT

At first, Zatt uses technology to locate the crystal for his lightsaber. Finally, he understands that he has to use the Force.

YOUNG BRAVERY

Armed with their new lightsabers, Zatt and his friends have to try and use everything they have learned to rescue Ahsoka Tano.

ZETT JUKASSA

JEDI RANK (J)

Youngling ☐
Padawan ☑
Knight ☐
Master ☐
Grand Master ☐

He might only be a Padawan, but Zett Jukassa has the courage and determination of a fully trained Jedi Knight. He is already a formidable warrior and will do anything he can to protect the Jedi Order.

JEDI FACT

Zett understands that a Jedi must study. When Obi-Wan visits the Jedi Archives to ask about Kamino, Zett is next in line to speak to the librarian.

Simple, gray robes

⊗ FIGHTING BACK

When Order 66 is activated, Zett doesn't hesitate. He bravely fights back against the clone troopers, although he is seriously outnumbered.

KEY FACTS

Homeworld: Unknown
Species: Human
Height: 1.57 m (5 ft 1 in)
Trained by: Unknown
Appearances: II, III

GLOSSARY

AMPHIBIOUS
Able to live on land and in water, such as a frog.

APPRENTICE
A person who is learning a skill.

AUTOPURSUIT
A mode on certain starfighters that allows them to chase and fire at targets without the pilot needing to do anything.

CLONE
An exact copy of another person.

CLONE WARS
A series of galaxy-wide battles between the Republic and the Separatists, who want to leave the Republic.

CLONE TROOPERS
Genetically identical humans who are soldiers for the Republic in the Clone Wars.

COMPASSIONATE
Feeling sympathy and concern for others.

CYBORG
A being who is part-organic and part-robot.

DARK SIDE
The part of the Force associated with hatred.

DROID
A kind of robot.

EMPIRE
The period when the galaxy is ruled by a single person, Emperor Palpatine. This Empire is ruled by fear and oppression.

FORCE
A natural and powerful energy that flows through all living things.

GALAXY
A group of millions of stars and planets.

IMPULSIVE
Acting without thinking first.

JEDI
A group that defends peace and justice in the galaxy.

JEDI CODE
The rules that the Jedi live by.

JEDI COUNCIL
A group of 12 Jedi Masters, led by the Grand Master, who work together to make decisions about the future of the Jedi.

JEDI TEMPLE
The Jedi headquarters, located on the planet Coruscant.

KYBER CRYSTAL
A crystal that channels energy and can be used to power a lightsaber.

LIGHTSABER
A Jedi or Sith's sword-like weapon, with a blade of glowing energy.

LIGHT SIDE
The part of the Force associated with peace, compassion, and healing.

MANIPULATE
To control or influence someone.

NOBLE
Showing great or unselfish personal qualities.

PATIENT
Being able to wait or accept delays without becoming angry or annoyed.

PROPHECY
A prediction of what is going to happen in the future.

REBELS
A collection of groups seeking to overthrow the Empire and restore the Republic.

RECKLESS
Not worrying about danger or the consequences of one's actions.

REDEEM
To make up for doing bad things.

REPUBLIC
Government of the galaxy by the people and their chosen (elected) representatives.

RESOURCEFUL
Finding quick or clever ways to solve problems.

RESPONSIBILITY
Having the duty or commitment to do something.

SACRIFICE
To give up something important or valuable for someone else, or to help someone else.

SENATOR
An elected representative of the government (Senate).

SCAVENGER
Someone who collects junk or other abandoned items to sell.

SITH
Enemies of the Jedi who use the dark side of the Force.

Senior Editor David Fentiman
Senior Designer Nathan Martin
Production Editor Marc Staples
Senior Production Controller Mary Slater
Managing Editor Emma Grange
Managing Art Editor Vicky Short
Publishing Director Mark Searle

For Lucasfilm
Senior Editor Brett Rector
Creative Director, Publishing Michael Siglain
Art Director Troy Alders
Story Group Leland Chee, Kate Izquierdo
Asset Management Sarah Williams, Elinor De La Torre,
Jackey Cabrera, and Shahana Alam
Special thanks to Scott Leong, Anthony Rodriguez,
and Angela Perez de Tagle

Designed for DK by Lisa Sodeau

First American Edition, 2022
Published in the United States by DK Publishing
1450 Broadway, Suite 801, New York, NY 10018

DK, a Division of Penguin Random House LLC
22 23 24 25 26 10 9 8 7 6 5 4 3 2 1
001–327238–May/2022

© & TM 2022 LUCASFILM LTD

Page design © 2022 Dorling Kindersley Limited

A catalog record for this book is available from
the Library of Congress.
ISBN 978-0-7440-5703-4

DK books are available at special discounts when purchased
in bulk for sales promotions, premiums, fund-raising,
or educational use.
For details, contact: DK Publishing Special Markets,
1450 Broadway, Suite 801, New York, NY 10018
SpecialSales@dk.com

Printed in Italy

For the curious

www.dk.com
www.starwars.com